TOTO
THE TORNADO
KITTEN

BY JONATHAN HALL

ILLUSTRATIONS BY CAROL RUZICKA

Toto
The Tornado
Kitten

by Jonathan Hall

Book design, layout, and all illustrations by Carol Ruzicka.

Story font set in Nobility Casual with Crumb as title and cover font.

Printed in the United States of America

For more information about this book visit www.Totothetornadokitten.com

Follow Toto on Facebook at TototheTornadoKitten

978-0-615-59101-8

First Edition **2012**

♥

This book is
for anyone
who has gone
out of their way
to help
an animal
in need.

♥

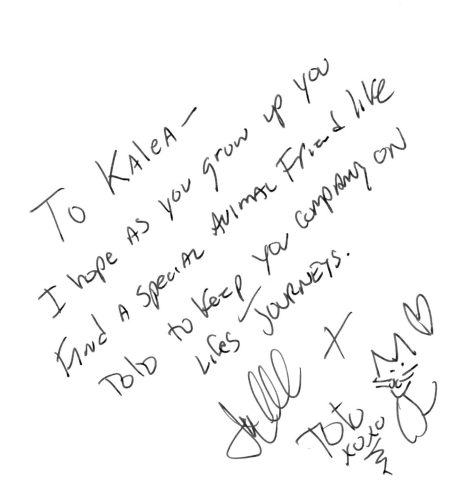

To KaleA —
I hope As you grow up you
Find A Special Animal Friend like
Toto to keep you company on
Lifes Journeys.

X

Toto xoxo

My name is Toto The Kitten.

I was born in the woods
in a town called Brimfield.

I lived happily in the woods and meadows with my mother.

One day a big storm
called a "tornado" came along.
The sky got darker...

and darker...

it started to rain...

and the wind began to blow.

It was so windy that I got blown all the way up into the top of a tree!

My home in the forest was gone. Lots of other people and animals lost their homes too. It was quite a mess.

"Meow" I cried out, "won't someone please come help me?"

It was getting dark and I was stuck in a tree.

A call was put out for help.

Ambulances. . .

fire trucks. . .

police cars. . .

and bucket
trucks rushed
to the scene.

A very nice man
who was helping to clean
up all the trees in the
forest found me.

I knew that I
would be OK!

He brought me to the fire station.
A special group of people were there,
helping all of the animals like me
who had lost their homes.

"Meow" I cried
out. I was so cold
and hungry.

I was taken
by the nice
people to a
special
hospital for
kittens far
away so
I could get
better.

I was so tiny
that I had to drink
milk from a
baby's bottle.

Next, I stayed at the animal shelter, a place for kittens like me who need a new home.

I began to grow and get bigger.

They were very, very nice to me.

I got to eat as much as I wanted.

I had *lots* of yummy food!

When people heard about my amazing story, they wrote me lots of letters and cards.

I was even on TV! I was a superstar.

Finally the day came when I was ready to leave. I had met lots of nice people, but I wanted a home I could call my own.

One day a nice couple came and chose me to go home with them, and guess what?

They took me back to Brimfield where my journey began.

Now each day in my
new home is fun
and exciting.

I chase cat toys. . .

I take
long naps. . .

and I love to sit on laps.

I get to go for car rides to see
my friend Doctor Michelle
at the animal hospital.

She makes sure that
I'm growing up to
be big and strong.

Sometimes, when its quiet and I'm alone at my new home, I get sad.

I miss my mom and my old home. I hope she knows I'm all right.

It's OK to miss the things you love. . .

But now I have a forever home
where I am very happy.

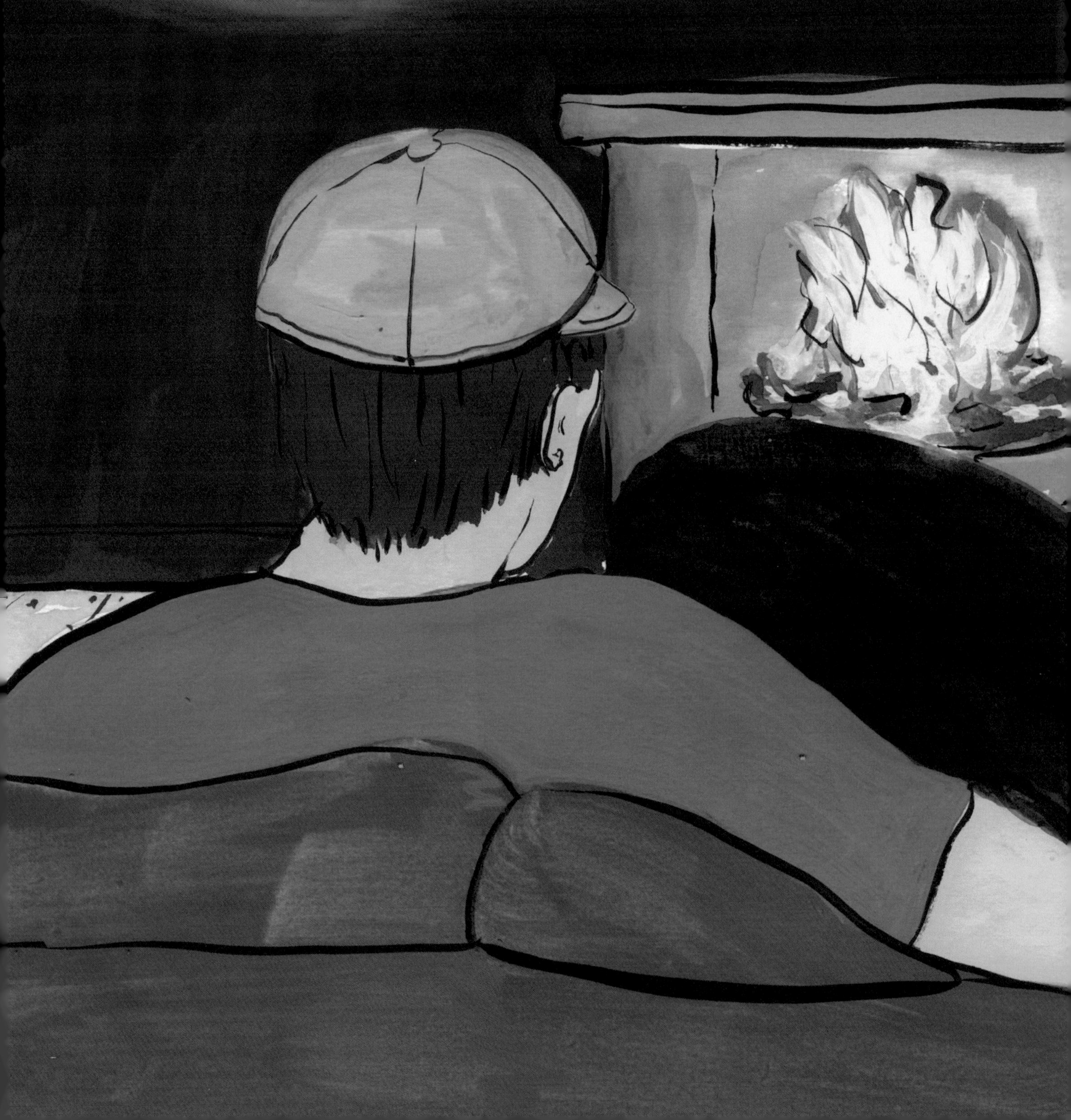

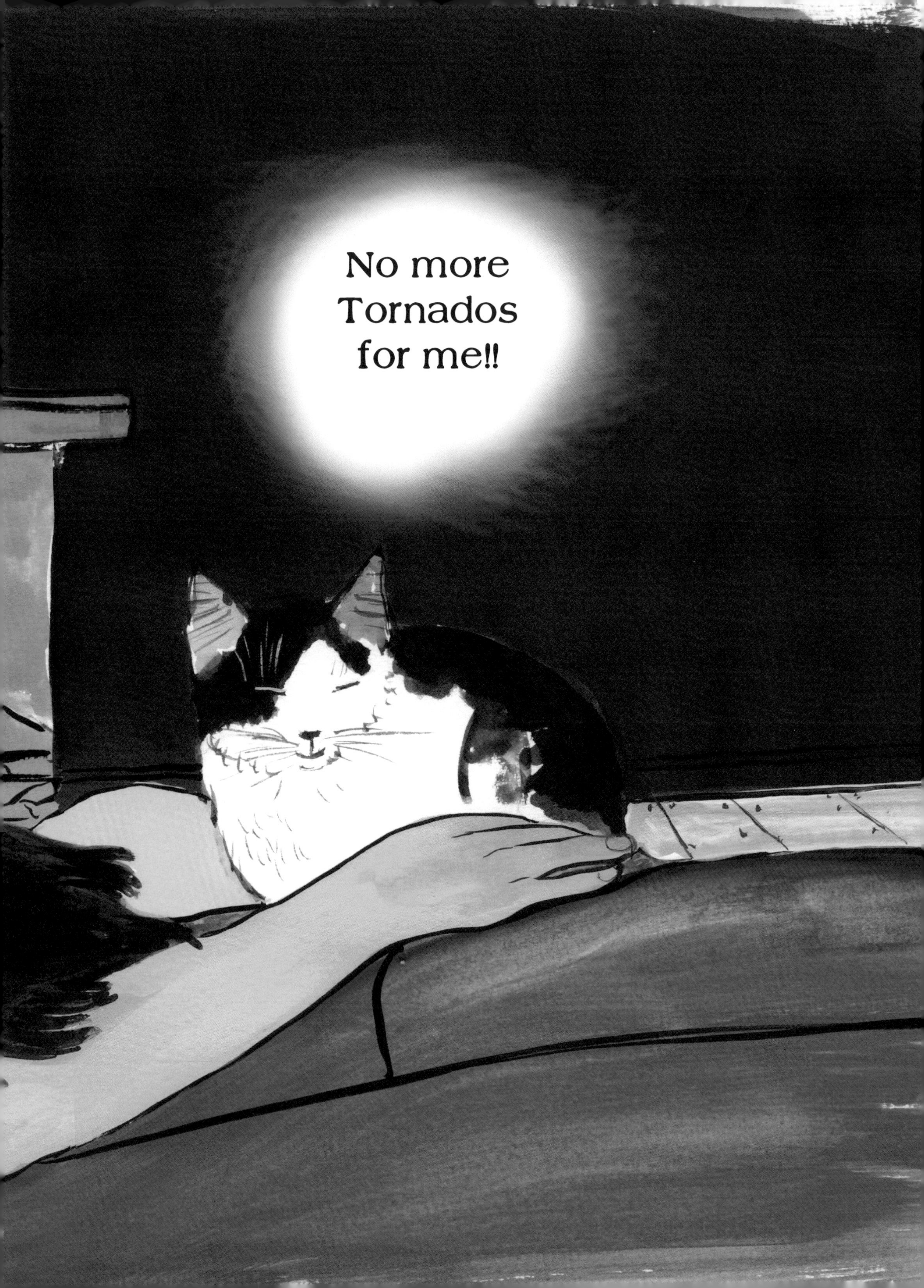
No more Tornados for me!!

About The Author:

This is Jonathan's first foray into the world of children's literature. Although initially an unlikely person for the job, his years of being an ambulance driver at an amusement park have made him truly understand the psyche of children. When not out kayaking, sailing, or lollygagging about, he is a Paramedic in his hometown of Brimfield, Massachusetts.

About Toto:

Toto the Kitten is doing well and now lives in Brimfield with the Author. His hobbies include chasing mice, eating assorted fruits, and taking long naps. He is looking forward to the accompanying book tour, so that he can meet lots of new friends and take trips in the car, a favorite pastime.

About The Illustrator:

Carol Ruzicka loves designing and illustrating for books and other print and web projects. She lives in the Green Mountains of Vermont. Visit her website at www.carolruzicka.com.

Prints of the artwork from this book
are available from the artist.
Contact her at her email address
ruzickacarol@gmail.com to order.

CPSIA information can be obtained
at www.ICGtesting.com
Printed in the USA
LVIC042028250312
274207LV00002BA